Tacos Anyone?

¿Alguien Quiere Tacos?

An Autism Story
Una Historia de Autismo

Written by / Escrito por
Marvie Ellis

Illustrated by / Ilustrado por
Jenny Loehr

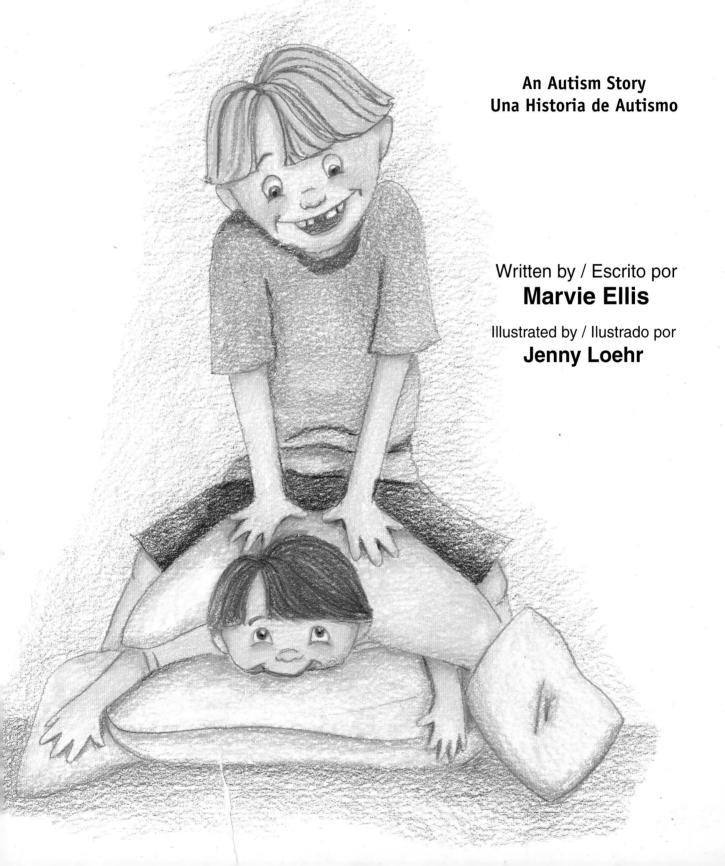

Disclaimer

This story herein is based on the author's extensive experience and knowledge. Readers should not attempt these therapy techniques without the supervision of, advice and training by qualified professionals.

Rectificación

Esta historia está basada en la extensa experiencia y conocimientos de la autora. Los amables lectores no deben de emprender estas técnicas de terapia sin la supervisión, consejo y entrenamiento de profesionales expertos.

Published in 2005 — **Second Printing 2007** — by Speech Kids Texas Press, Inc.,
3802 Beaconsdale Drive
Austin, Texas 78727

ISBN: 978-1-933319-02-5 — Hardback
(10-digit ISBN#—1-933319-02-X)
Library of Congress Card Number: 2005901420

Ellis, Marvie
Tacos Anyone? / written by Marvie Ellis; illustrated by Jenny Loehr.
1 st. ed. - Austin, Texas.:
Speech Kids Texas Press, Inc., © 2005.
32 p.: col. Ill.; 29 cm.
An Autism Story
Summary: Michael is a four year old boy with autism. His older brother, Thomas, doesn't understand why Michael behaves the way he does. The therapist teaches Thomas how to play with Michael, making sibling time fun again.
1. Autism - Juvenile fiction. 2. Siblings - Juvenile fiction. 3. Sensory/ Play - Juvenile fiction.
4. Therapist - Juvenile fiction. 5. Spanish Translation - Juvenile fiction.
6. Multicultural - Juvenile fiction 1. Loehr, Jenny, ill. II. Title.
First Edition. Text Copyright © 2005 by Marvie Ellis.
Illustrations Copyright © 2005 by Jenny Loehr.

For inquiries about the author and information about
Speech Kids Texas Press, Inc., please visit our website at

www.speechkidstexaspress.com

Rita Mills—Book Packaging Consultant—The Book Connection
Victor Higginbotham—Cover Design

The paper used in this publication meets the requirements of the American National Standard
for Permanence of Paper for Printed Library Materials Z39.48 1984.
Printed in China

Acknowledgements

Thank you my husband, Tellis and son, Brian for your love, support and patience. I love you very much.

Thank you my mentor / sister / friend, Karla Frazier, D.M.D., in Austin, for your tremendous encouragement and my bright teeth.
Thank you my sister, Lynn Harris and family for letting me read to you over the phone past bedtime.
Thank you my brother, Calvin Frazier, for being a great soundboard.
Thank you Mom (Mrs. Marvie Frazier) for without whom none of my business dreams could have been.
Thank you, Grandmas Tommie & MaMas, Grandpa Georgie, and my father-in-law, T.B. Ellis, III, M.D., for your daily prayers and encouragement.
Thank you, Dolly for your editing skills.
Thank you, Mrs. Maria L. Cruz for translating the stories.
Thank you very much, Mrs. Tayde Gladyn for your extra help with Spanish translation and editing skills.
Thank you, Jenny for having a special gift and sharing it with me. Thank you, Lavelle Carlson for being a role model.
Thank you, Rita Mills for your time, advice and contributions.
Thanks to all the parents and professionals who took the time and care to review the stories.

Most of all, thank you to all the children with ASD, you are most inspiring.

In remembrance of my father, Henry C. Frazier, Ph.D.
I love and miss you deeply.
May God bless and keep us.

Foreword

This collection of stories is a reflection of the importance of understanding the diversity of individuals with autism. In this ground-breaking series, many nuances of autism are explored. Perspectives from parents and siblings are provided. These heart warming short stories are useful for anyone who interacts with those with autism.

This is the first time a series of books has been presented specifically on autism in a short, easy to read, and dual language format. The format allows for quick reading with just enough information to spark the desire for further exploration. These books are beneficial to anyone who deals with individuals who have autism of any age. They can be useful for teachers, day care providers, students, medical professionals, psychologists, occupational therapists, physical therapists, speech-language pathologists, administrators, ministers, bus drivers, etc. People with autism are becoming more involved in the community, and the importance of a basic understanding, or at least some familiarity with this condition is necessary.

It is my hope, that this series of books is just the beginning of a whole new wave of consciousness as it relates to individuals with disabilities. It is so rewarding to see a series of stories that is so beneficial to many people, yet simple enough to facilitate basic understanding of such a complex condition. The inclusion of therapeutic techniques offers a unique and indirect perspective of the many facets of autism. These stories are definitely worth reading.

LaQuinta Khaldun, M.S., CCC-SLP
Speech-Language Pathologist/ Owner
Carolina Speech Services
Charlotte, NC

Tacos Anyone?

¿Alguien Quiere Tacos?

Hi. I'm Thomas and this is my little brother, Michael. Michael is four years old and has autism.

Hola. Soy Tomas y este es mi pequeño hermano, Miguel. Miguel tiene cuatro años y tiene autismo.

I don't know what autism really means. My mom says it just means that Michael needs more help listening, learning, and playing.

Yo no sé realmente lo que es autismo. Mi mamá dice que esto solo significa que Miguel necesita más ayuda para escuchar, aprender y jugar.

Michael doesn't like to play with me much. When I try to play next to him, he gets up and walks away.

A Miguel no le gusta jugar mucho conmigo. Cuando trato de jugar al lado de el, el se levanta y se aleja.

FINGER PAINTS

He likes jumping and playing with his cars. He will jump up and down on his bed for an hour if he gets really excited.

Le gusta brincar y jugar con sus carros. Si se emociona mucho da brincos en su cama por una hora.

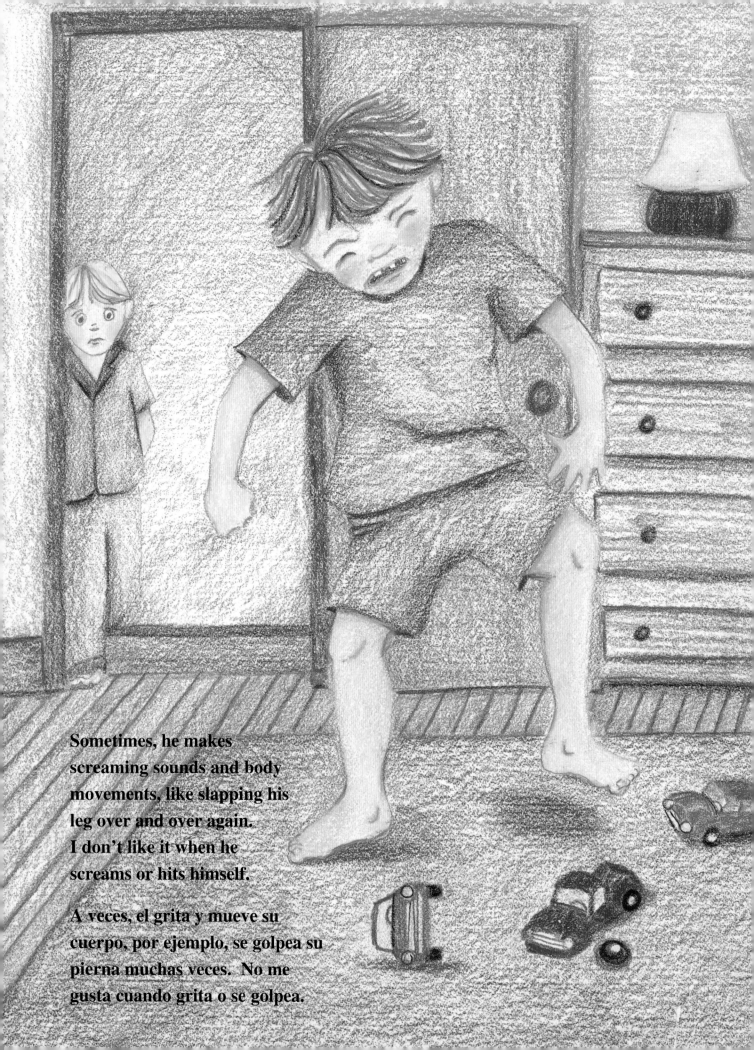

Sometimes, he makes
screaming sounds and body
movements, like slapping his
leg over and over again.
I don't like it when he
screams or hits himself.

A veces, el grita y mueve su
cuerpo, por ejemplo, se golpea su
pierna muchas veces. No me
gusta cuando grita o se golpea.

Mom says he's trying to tell us something
and we should listen.

Mamá dice que el trata
de decirnos
algo y debemos
escucharlo.

Michael goes to see his therapist, Ms. Karla. She helps kids with listening, learning, and playing. They get to do really neat things. She bounces him on a big red bouncy ball,

Miguel visita a su terapeuta llamada, Sra. Karla. Ella ayuda a niños a escuchar, aprender, y jugar. Hacen muchas cosas muy bonitas. Ella lo pone a brincar en una pelota roja y grande,

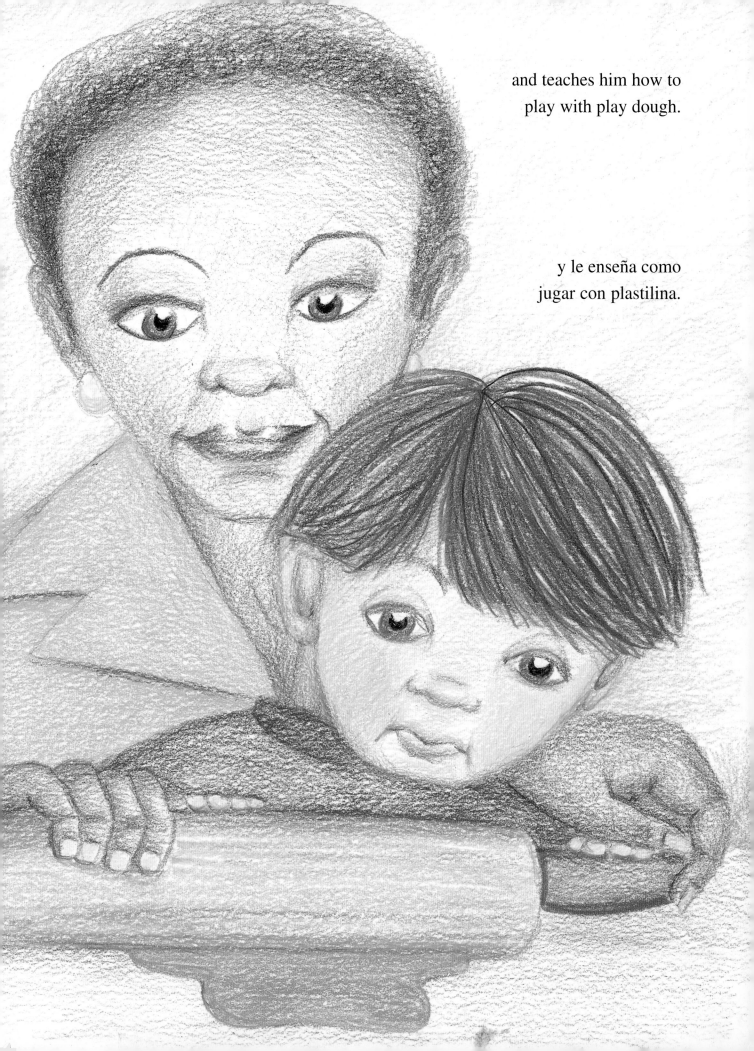

and teaches him how to
play with play dough.

y le enseña como
jugar con plastilina.

Ms. Karla also teaches
him sign language.

La Sra. Karla también le
enseña lenguaje de
señales.

mother

madre

Ms. Karla helps him blow bubbles
and whistles. She says it
makes his mouth
stronger.

La Sra. Karla le ayuda a soplar burbujas
y a silbar. Ella dice que esto hace su
boca más fuerte.

Ms. Karla invites me to play with them when I come
to her office. She says, "Thomas, if we
watch Michael carefully, we can
see whether or not he
likes something."

La Sra. Karla me invita a jugar con ellos cuando
vengo a su oficina. Ella dice, "Tomas, si miramos
a Miguel con cuidado, podemos ver si algo le
gusta o no le gusta."

They play with
macaroni
noodles
and have
great
snacks.

Juegan con fideos de macarron
y comen alimentos muy buenos.

She showed me how Michael frowns and
walks away when she gets out the paints
for finger painting. I didn't know he
doesn't like wet paint on his hands.

Ella me mostró como
Miguel frunce el ceño y
se aleja cuando ella
saca las pinturas para
pintar con los dedos.
Yo no sabia que no le
gusta la pintura en sus
manos.

When she brought out puzzles, Michael sat
down at the table waiting for her.
He must like puzzles.

Cuando ella sacó los rompecabezas, Miguel
se sentó a la mesa esperando por ella. A él le
gustan los rompecabezas.

Michael's favorite thing is when Ms. Karla makes a taco out of him by rolling him up in a large egg crate mattress pad. He always laughs when they do that!

La cosa favorita de Miguel es cuando la Sra. Karla lo hace un taco enrollándolo con un colchón grande. ¡El siempre se ríe cuando ellos hacen esto!

Yesterday, I was at home and noticed Michael pulling
our big pillows off our sofa.

Ayer, estaba en casa y noté, que Miguel sacó las
almohadas grandes de nuestro sofá.

I was about to tell him to stop, when I remembered
what Ms. Karla said about watching his
face and body movements.

Estuve a punto de decirle que no hiciera
eso, cuando recordé lo que la Sra. Karla
dijo sobre la mirada de su cara y
movimientos de su cuerpo.

I stood next to Michael and
asked, "Do you want a taco?"

Me puse de pie al lado de Miguel y le
pregunté, "¿Quieres un taco?"

He turned, looked at me, and said, "Tado!"

Se volteó, me miró, y dijo "¡Tado!"

I was very happy! I yelled, "Mom, come and see what we made!"

¡Me puse muy feliz! Grité, "¡Mamá, venga a ver lo que hicimos!"

It was the first time Michael and I had played together in a long time.

Esta fue la primera vez que Miguel y yo
jugamos juntos en mucho tiempo.

Last night, I made 20 tacos.

Anoche, hice 20 tacos.

Parent Reviews

"Very sweet story of an older sibling trying for that interaction that comes so naturally for 'normal developing siblings.'"

—*Lisa B. (son with ASD)*

"The beauty of these stories is to encourage family members to learn and practice doing 'therapy' at home. It helps young kids to understand the world of autistic children."

—*Cuc N. (daughter & son with ASD)*

"I love the simplicity of the text and ideas and think they would be a great tool for teaching empathy and understanding to peers and family members. Well done, Marvie!"

—*Michelle S. (son with ASD)*

Comentarios de Padres de Familia

"Una historia muy dulce de un hermano mayor tratando de aspirar a aquella interacción, lo cual es muy fácil con 'hermanos de desarrollo normales.'"

—*Lisa B. (hijo tiene ASD)*

"La belleza de estas historias debe animar a miembros de familia a aprender y practicar haciendo 'la terapia' en casa. Esto ayuda a niños jóvenes a entender el mundo de niños autistas.»

—*Cuc N. (hija e hijo tienen ASD)*

"Amo la simplicidad del texto e ideas y pienso que ellos serían un gran instrumento para enseñar la empatía y entendimiento a amigos y familiares. ¡Bien hecho, Marvie!"

—*Michele S. (hijo tiene ASD)*

Professional Reviews

"The stories are great....They are clever and intriguing."

—*Chris P. Johnson, M.Ed., M.D.,*
American Academy of Pediatrics (AAP) Committee on
Children with Disabilities and co-chair of the AAP
Autism Expert Panel; Clinical Professor of Pediatrics at
the Health Science Center at the University of Texas at
San Antonio, and founder of CAMP (the Children's
Association for Maximal Potential)

"My favorite of all of your stories. It explains some of the challenges for a child with autism in such a clear manner for a sibling to understand."

—*Lori Hickman, M.S.,*
OTR/L, SIPT Certification #1528, STARS (Student
Therapies And Resource Services), Phoenix, AZ

". . . factually accurate story of a child with autism. It explains, in understandable terms, some of the behaviors that serve a communicative purpose that would otherwise seem annoying or rude to people. The story is very realistic, celebrating specific achievements in our understanding of autism, not unrealistic fairytale endings. The role of a therapist is explained very well with specific examples. This is a very touching story."

—*Kapila Seshadri, M.D.,*
Associate Professor of Pediatrics, Section Head,
Section of NeuroDevelopmental Disabilities, Department
of Pediatrics, UMDNJ—Robert Wood Johnson
Medical School, New Jersey

"[This story] for family members [was] delightful. I especially liked how [it] gave useful tips for coping with the unique problems that can develop when a sibling or family member has autism."

– *Barbara A. Booth, Ph.D., BCBA, Director*
of Special Education, Pflugerville, Texas ISD

"I would de̶̶itely consider them for purchase as there seems to ̶̶ paucity of books to read to young children ̶̶nks again for making the effort to supply ̶̶"

Janne Zochert, Education Coordinator,
̶d Start, Williamson-Burnet County, Texas

"This is a nicely written and wonderfully illustrated story about a child with autism from the perspective of a sibling. The child's brother describes his brother's behaviors including sensory-based problems. Through this story, his brother learns from a therapist how to interact with his brother and is elated in his ability to play with him for the first time. This is a 'must have' resource for teachers and parents to read to peers and siblings."

—*Hope Korbet, M.S., CCC-SLP,*
Kennedy Krieger Institute, Center for Autism and Related
Disorders, Baltimore, MD

"This story is sensitive, and unique portrayal of the social weaknesses seen in children with autism spectrum disorders. I enjoyed the uplifting ending as well as the colorful illustration."

—*Christine T. Barry, Ph.D., Pediatric Neuropsychologist, Associate Professor of Pediatrics, Division of Behavioral Pediatrics and Psychology, Case Western University, School of Medicine, Cleveland, OH*

Comentarios Profesionales

"Las historias son muy buenas.... Son ingeniosas e intrigantes."

—*Chris P. Johnson, M.Ed., M.D., Academia Americana de Pediatría (AAP) Comité para Niños Deshabilitados y co-presidente del Jurado Experto en Autismo; Profesor de la Clínica en Pediatría del Centro de Ciencias Médicas en la Universidad de Texas de San Antonio, y miembro fundador de CAMP (The Children's Association for Maximal Potential—La Asociación de Potencial Máximo Para Niños)*

"De todas sus historias es mi favorita. Explica algunos desafíos para un niño con autismo de una manera tan clara que los hermanos puedan entender."

—*Lori Hickman, M.S., OTR/L. Certificación SIPT No. 1528, STARS (Student Therapies and Resource Services—*Terapias de Estudiantes y Servicios en Recursos.)* Phoenix, AZ*

"Este libro es muy fácil de leer, y es una historia verdadera de un niño con autismo. Esto explica, en términos comprensibles, algunos comportamientos que sirven un objetivo comunicativo que les pueden parecer a las personas como molestos o groseros. La historia es muy realista, celebrando logros específicos en nuestro entendimiento de autismo, sin finales de cuentos de hadas no realistas. El papel de un terapeuta es explicado muy bien con ejemplos específicos. Esta es una historia muy conmovedora."

—*Kapila Seshadri, M.D., Profesor Asociado de Pediatría, Director de Sección, Sección de Deshabilidades de NeuroDesarrollo, Departamento de Pediatría, UMDNJ—Robert Wood Johnson Medical School, New Jersey*

"[Esta historia] para miembros de familia [fue] encantadora. Sobre todo me gustaron las recomendaciones, dio útiles puntos para enfrentarse con los problemas que resultan cuando un hermano o miembro de la familia tiene autismo."

—*Barbara A. Booth, Ph.D., BCBA, Directora de Educación Especial, Distrito Escolar Independiente de Pflugerville, Texas*

"Considero que definitivamente los compraría ya que parece haber una falta de libros para leer a niños pequeños... De nuevo, gracias por esforzarse en abastecer esta demanda."

—*Janne Zochert, Coordinadora de Educación, Head Start, Williamson-Burnet County, Texas*

"Esta historia reconoce la realidad multifacética de autismo. Demostrando como se le permite al hermano estar involucrado en la terapia es muy positivo. La historia describe como los hermanos pueden tomar una parte integral en el proceso de comunicación. También demuestra como los hermanos desean aprender y ayudar."

—*LaQuinta Khaldun, M.S., CCC-SLP, dueña de Carolina Speech Services, North Carolina*

"Esta historia está bien escrita y maravillosamente ilustrada sobre un niño autista desde la perspectiva de un familiar. El hermano del niño describe el comportamiento de su hermano incluyendo los problemas sensoriales. A través de esta historia, el hermano aprende como una terapeuta interactúa con su hermano y está encantado de poder jugar con él por primera vez. Es un libro que todos los profesores y padres deben de tener y leer con sus amigos y familiares."

—*Hope Korbet, M.S., CCC-SLP, Instituto Kennedy Krieger, Centro para Autismo y Deshabilidades Relacionadas con el Autismo, Baltimore, MD*

"Esta historia es la representación sensible, y única de las debilidades sociales vistas en niños con desórdenes de espectro de autismo. Disfruté del gran final inspirado así como las vistosas ilustraciones."

—*Christine T. Barry, Ph.D., Neuropsicologa de Pediatría, Profesora Asociada en Pediatría, Departamento de Comportamiento y Psicología Pediátrica, Case Western University, Escuela de Medicina, Cleveland, OH*

About the Author:

Marvie Ellis received her Bachelor of Science degree in Communicative Disorders from Jackson State University in Jackson, Mississippi and her Master of Science degree from the University of North Carolina at Chapel Hill (1996). She has specialized training in working with the birth to five population, children with autism spectrum disorders, speech-language delays, oral motor therapy, play based therapy, sensory therapy, and behavior modification techniques. Marvie provides trainings and seminars to parents and educators nationally. She is a member of the American Speech-Language and Hearing Association, the Texas Speech-Language and Hearing Association, and the Autism Society of America. Marvie lives in Austin with her husband, Tellis and son, Brian. She enjoys writing stories, supporting others in their entrepreneurial and quiet moments for meditation.

Sobre La Autora:

Marvie Ellis obtuvo su Licenciatura en Ciencias en Desórdenes de Comunicación de la Universidad de Jackson en Jackson, Mississippi y su Maestría de Licenciatura en Ciencias de la Universidad de Carolina del Norte en Chapel Hill (1996). Se ha especializado trabajando con niños que tienen desórdenes de autismo, habla y lenguaje retrasado, terapia de motor oral, terapia basada en juegos, terapia sensorial, y técnicas modificando comportamientos de niños desde su nacimiento hasta los cinco años. Marvie es una altavoz nacional y asesora de padres y educadores. Es miembro de la Asociación Americana del Habla y Lenguaje, Asociación de Texas del Habla-Lenguaje y Oído y la Sociedad de Autismo de America. Marvie vive en Austin con su esposo, Tellis e hijo, Brian. Le gusta escribir historias, para ayudar a personas en sus ocupaciones y momentos de meditación.

About the Illustrator:

Jenny Loehr obtained her Master of Arts degree in Speech Pathology in northern California at Humboldt State University in 1990. She has been practicing art and illustration three times as long as she has been a clinician, and recently been able to "marry" the two professions by opening Curly Girl Studios where she illustrates books and materials for the speech-language pathology and audiology community. Jenny spends her days illustrating and practicing speech pathology in Austin, Texas where she lives with her husband Brian, and her two boys, Jacob and Joshua.

Sobre La Ilustradora:

Jenny Loehr obtuvo su Maestría de Arte en Patología del Habla en la Universidad Humboldt en el Norte de California en 1990. Ha ejercido su arte e ilustración tres veces más tiempo que el tiempo que ha ejercido en clínicas, y recientemente ha podido combinar sus dos profesiones en sus Curly Girl Studios, ilustrando libros y documentos para la comunidad especializada en patología del habla-lenguaje y audiología. Jenny pasa sus días ilustrando y practicando patología del habla en Austin, Texas, donde vive con su esposo Brian, y sus dos hijos, Jacob y Joshua.